THE
FRIDAY PARCEL

For my godson, Matthew Prior,
with much love

Matt stared down the lane and
watched the bus with Mum in it
turn into a little red dot. He felt
sad. Gran-in-the-town was ill in
bed, and needed looking after.
So Matt was staying with Gran-
in-the-country, all on his own.

  'Don't do anything *I* wouldn't
do!' Mum shouted, through the

window. And the bus disappeared. Well, *that* was all right. She did funny things sometimes, when she got muddled. Like going to the postbox in her nightie, and meeting his teacher, Miss Glover. And she'd once put his beans in the dustbin, and not on his toast!

'Come on,' said Gran. 'Cheer up. Your dinner's ready. It's fish and chips today.'

Matt followed her across the farmyard. He liked it at Gran's. She had cows and sheep, and a very old donkey called Thistle. There were cats and dogs too, and some fussy brown hens.

Gran did funny things as well. You'd expect that, because she

was Mum's mum. And she had
lots of different hats for all the
different jobs she did, around
the farm. Gran could be fun.

But it wasn't going to be fun
this time, Matt decided. Not all
on his own.

An aeroplane flew low, over
the fields, and the whirring noise
made the donkey hee-haw
crossly. Thistle had bad moods,
and he didn't like loud noises
while he was eating. He shook
his floppy ears, and stamped.

'I wish it was Dad, flying home
for dinner,' thought Matt. But
Dad was away in the Air Force,
trying out new planes. The
sound made him feel lonelier.

In bed that night Matt heard more planes come over. He had a strange dream about Mum, Dad and Gran, flying round the sky in a big red bus, with wings.

At breakfast next day he wrote 'Mum' on his porridge, in syrup.

'How long is a week?' he asked Mr Stanley, the odd job man. Mr Stanley talked in grunts and smoked a pipe. He had an old woolly hat but Gran had borrowed it, to put on the tea-pot. She liked her tea hot.

'Seven days,' he grunted. 'But your mum may be back on Friday.'

'And what's today?'

'Monday, lad.'

Five whole days before Matt
saw Mum again.

'Don't mope,' said Gran,
whisking away the tablecloth.
'Look for your parcel. There'll
be one every day, if you're good.
Some boys are lucky.'

His *parcel*? Nobody had
mentioned parcels before. What
could Gran mean? She was
outside now, pegging washing
on the line. It was windy so she
wore a bright red bobble hat, to
keep her ears warm. A parcel...
Matt was going to look for it. At
once.

First he looked under the
table, then behind the chest.
Then behind the dresser and

under the carpet. Cooper,
Gran's fat ginger cat, was just
like a parcel himself, all neat on
his chair, but Matt didn't dare
move *him*. He sometimes had
rages, and bit people.

Cooper was the Inside cat. He

lived in the kitchen and ate up
all the scraps. The Outside one,
Mrs Cat, was peeping through
the window, watching Matt
hunt. She'd got three kittens and
lived in the red barn.

Matt thought it was silly to
call her Mrs Cat. She *was* a cat,
anyway. 'It's not silly at all,' said
Gran. 'I've had so many cats
I've quite run out of names.'

It took ages to find the
Monday parcel, then...BINGO!
There it was! Up on the dresser,
inside a blue dish. It was a giant
water pistol, and the label said
'Shoots Ten Metres'.

Gran frowned when she saw
what was inside the wrapping

paper. She knew all about boys with water pistols.

'Keep it away from my washing,' she said. 'It's a good drying day.'

But Matt fired water everywhere.

Cooper got wet, disappeared under the table, and hissed so hard that Matt ran off outside. Thistle got wet too, and marched off to sulk, in the brambles. Mrs Cat rushed into the barn and hid her three kittens under some straw, and Mr Stanley's pipe went out, with a fizzling noise.

'You could water my beans with that, I reckon,' he grunted, wiping his glasses.

On Tuesday morning Gran told Matt to look in the Very Best Room. She'd been dusting and she had a bright yellow scarf wound round and round her head. She looked like an Indian Prince.

Matt lifted up fat cushions and peered through curly table legs.

No parcel.

Gran unlocked the door of the grandfather clock and he looked in there.

No parcel.

'Try the rug,' she suggested. 'It might be a flat sort of parcel today.' So Matt burrowed underneath like a mole, with his bottom in the air.

Still no parcel.

Then he spotted it, perched on
top of a china dog. It looked
little, round, and boring.

Matt grabbed it and tore off
the paper. It was a coloured box
with holes in. If you turned it

over, very slowly, it made a loud
mooing noise.

Gran jumped. 'Ugh!' she said.
'I don't want cows in my Very
Best Room, *or* in my kitchen.
I've got enough with cats and
washing. Take it outside, Matt.'
So he did.

He went into the field and
played it to the new calves.
They sidled up very close, then
their mother arrived and shooed
them away. She didn't trust that
cow thing at all.

Nor did Cooper. He spat at it,
through the window, and the
hens all flapped round and ran
off to hide, under the tractor.

The Wednesday parcel caused

trouble. Matt hunted for hours before he found it. Then he saw something, wrapped in blue paper. It was high up on a shelf, behind Gran's drying rack.

The rack was fixed to the kitchen ceiling with ropes, and it was full of clean clothes.

CRASH! Matt reached right up and down came the rack. Shirts fell all over the floor and a pair of stripy knickers landed on Gran's head. She did look funny!

'You should have waited, Matt,' she said. 'I'd have got it down for you.'

She tugged on the ropes and the rack went up to the ceiling again, with a squeaky noise.

Then she picked up her iron and set to work. She didn't seem to notice the knickers.

Inside the blue paper Matt found a joke book. He started to read it to Gran but she was hot and bothered. She didn't like Terrible Jokes when she was ironing.

'Gran, how does an elephant get down from a tree?'

'I don't know, I'm sure,' she said.

'It sits on a leaf, and waits for Autumn.'

'I see.' (The knickers had slipped to one side now, and she looked like a pirate.)

'Gran, what's yellow and goes "buzz-buzz"?'

'I couldn't think.'

'Supersonic custard.'

'Matt, I—oh, look at that!' There was a big black singe on her best white sheet. 'Off you go!' she said crossly.

Matt crept outside and read his book to Mr Stanley as he watered his garden. The old man sucked on his pipe and gave a grunty kind of laugh at the one about the custard. He quite liked the Terrible Jokes.

So did Thistle.

When he saw Matt he 'hee-hawed' loudly and came running over. This boy sometimes brought him carrots.

They stared at one another, through the fence. Then Thistle yawned, showing rows and rows of great big teeth. Matt stepped back, dropping the Terrible Jokes, and the donkey bent his shaggy grey head and ATE

them, Chomp, Chomp, Chomp.
There was nothing left at all!

The Thursday parcel was
nowhere to be found. Matt
looked in every place he could
think of, and every place was
empty.

Nobody helped. Mr Stanley
was too busy in his vegetable
plot and Gran was up a ladder,
picking apples. She wore a big
black hat with a wide brim. She
looked a bit like a cowboy.

At bedtime Matt went upstairs
miserably, all alone. He got
undressed and kicked his shoes
under the bed. There it was,
staring out at him, a monster
mask with green hair! It had

pointy teeth and a long, long
nose.

Matt stretched out his arm,
but couldn't quite reach it. So he
lay down flat and crawled under
the bed. But there wasn't much
room, and he got caught in some
rusty springs. He wriggled and

jiggled and tried to get free, but the harder he tried the worse it was. He was soon stuck fast!

Matt didn't like it under that bed. There were cobwebs, so there were bound to be spiders too. He grabbed the mask and gave a last big wriggle.

R-I-P! that was his pyjama

jacket. T-E-A-R! That was his
pyjama pants.

But Matt was free, and he
slithered out, all covered with
dust.

He put his mask on straight
away, and stuck his head

35

through the open window. 'Hey!'
he yelled.

Mr Stanley was still in his
vegetable plot. When he saw the
great green face he dropped his
hoe and fell down flat, among
the cabbages. The calves all ran

off, in a mooing huddle, and
Mrs Cat leapt up the apple tree
and sat there, peeping through
the leaves.

Gran was still up the ladder.
As Mrs Cat whizzed past she
dropped her basket and all the
apples fell into the grass. Plonk.
Plonk. Then her cowboy hat
flew off, and sailed across the
fields like a big black bat.

The mask was back under the
bed when she came up to say
good night to Matt. And he was
pretending to be asleep.

The Friday parcel must have
vanished into thin air. He hunted
all morning and all afternoon. Mr
Stanley couldn't help, he was

too busy weeding, and Matt
didn't like to ask Gran. She had
found the rips in his pyjamas.

Her needle and thread flashed
in and out, and she frowned
behind her spectacles. She wore a
little brown hood buttoned under
her chin, to keep the spectacles
on her nose. The sewing hat
made her look just like a pixie.

'I can't find it anywhere,'
Matt said at last. 'Will you help
me, Gran?'

'Wait and see,' she replied.
And at that very moment there
was a great big BANG on the
kitchen door.

'Parcel Post!' someone shouted.
That was odd. The postman

always knocked at the front, and
he never came at teatime.

Matt went outside and nearly
fell over the thing that was
blocking the doorway. In the
middle of the step was a huge
cardboard box, but whoever had
brought it had disappeared.

'Washing Machine' said the
letters on the side, and the label
said 'Matt Prior, Overton Farm'.

Gran came out. '*I* don't need
a washing machine,' she said.
Neither did Matt. He liked
getting dirty. What could it
mean?

He looked carefully all round
the farmyard. Thistle was
peering at him, over the fence.

Perhaps he was hoping for carrots, or some more Terrible Jokes. The brown hens fussed around Gran's feet. It was long past their teatime.

Mrs Cat had crept up to the big box and was pawing at it,

gently. Then Cooper stalked out of his kitchen, jumped on top, and hissed.

Mrs Cat fled, back to her kittens in the old red barn, and Cooper stood there, like a big furry statue. After a minute he started to sniff at the box too.

It wasn't very well packed. there was no sticky tape, and no string, and the pieces on top were flapping about in the wind. Cooper took a big bite.

The parcel moved slightly, and Matt and his grandmother looked at one another. What could be in there?

Cooper sniffed harder, then clawed at the box with a big ginger paw.

The huge parcel wobbled about, then started to bulge. Cooper jumped off and ran into his kitchen.

Then, quite suddenly, the top flaps opened and up popped...
MUM!

'Now I know what a washing machine feels like,' she laughed, climbing out of the box.

Matt didn't laugh, he just stared. He couldn't quite believe it, not yet. But they were soon in the kitchen, having cups of tea. (Mr Stanley's woolly hat kept the pot warm.)

'Did you like all your parcels?' asked Mum.

'I liked the water pistol, and the mask. But I ripped my pyjamas under the bed. And Mr Stanley fell over, and Gran burned her sheet. And Thistle *ate* those Terrible Jokes.'

'I liked everything really,' he said at last, 'But the Friday

parcel was the best thing of all.'
And he gave her a very big
hug.

THE
JUNGLE SALE

For Flute

Matt felt excited. He was going to
his very first jungle sale and he
was planning to buy a lion.

Mum said you could get things
quite cheap at jungle sales but
Matt had been saving up in
secret. If there was only one lion,
everyone might want it. It would
cost a lot then.

The money from the sale was going to buy a new climbing frame for the church playgroup. Their house was next to the church hall so Mum was helping. People kept dumping boxes outside their front door, then ringing the bell and going away.

'Is that for the sale too?' Matt said one tea-time, when another big box appeared on the doorstep. He could see an old sock poking out of the top.

'Yes, and it'll have to go up here.'

Mum climbed on to the kitchen table to reach a high shelf.

'Why do they sell socks at jungle sales?' Matt had hoped the

box might have a monkey in it, or
a parrot, or even a slimy, slithery
snake.

But Mum wasn't really
listening. She was too busy
moving old jam jars to make
room for the box. 'Oh, they sell all
sorts of things,' she called down.
'Somebody's sure to buy these
socks. You wait and see.'

Socks! How boring, when you
could buy a lion, thought Matt.

'What do they eat?' he said.

'What do what eat?' Mum gave
a great big sneeze. The jam jars
were very dusty.

'Lions, when they're babies?'

'Oh, milk I suppose, and scraps,
till they get their big teeth. Now,

what's all this about lions when
I'm trying to find a place for all
these socks and vests?'

'Oh, nothing,' said Matt, and
he went out to play.

His lion was going to live in the
old broken-down shed at the
bottom of the garden, and he
would feed it when nobody was
looking.

When it got a bit bigger he
might tell people the secret. Then
Dad could make a run for it, so it
could get some fresh air. Dad was
very good at making things.

The week before the sale, Mum
was very busy, and a bit grumpy
too. The house was so full of

boxes you could hardly move.

There were boxes in the bedrooms and boxes in the kitchen.

Big boxes in the hall and little boxes all the way up the stairs.

They were definitely running out of room!

'I'll be glad when the playgroup people have taken all this away,' Mum said, tripping over a box as she ran to answer the front door bell. 'In fact, I'll be glad when this sale's over and done with.'

So will I, thought Matt. I'll have my lion then.

He'd already cleared a space
for it in the shed and he'd saved
up quite a few scraps for it too,
half a sausage, some crisps and a
peanut butter sandwich.

'Will everything be in cages?' he
asked Mum, thinking about all
the different animals at the jungle
sale.

'In cages?' His mother laughed.
'Not unless someone's given us a
rabbit, or some white mice. This
box seems to be old shoes,
mainly,' she muttered, pulling
things out if it.

'Aren't there any animals at
all?' Matt said.

'Well, there's a snake here.
Catch!' And she threw a long
wiggly thing at him.

Matt jumped, then stared. It
was made of old green blanket
and all the stuffing was coming
out. 'Gran's got one of those,'
he said, 'to stop the cold air
coming under the door.'

'Don't you want it then?'

'No!'

So the snake went back in its
baked beans carton, with the
shoes.

On the night before the jungle
sale, Matt couldn't get to sleep.
He kept thinking about his lion,
and whether he'd got enough
money saved up.

When he did doze off he had a horrid dream. There was a lion for sale, a really huge one. It had big flashing eyes and a great shaggy mane and it sat in a golden cage in the middle of the church hall. Everyone was crowding round to look at it.

Matt got to the front by pushing his way through people's legs. He held his money out but the lady in charge told him that the price was One Million Pounds.

The lion was bought by a big fat man who smoked smelly cigars. He left a million pound coins in a shiny heap on the floor, then he went off. He had ordered

two servants to come and take the lion away in a trailer. It was going to do clever tricks in his circus.

When the lion heard this a big tear rolled down its cheek. Matt cried too.

At breakfast, Mum changed her kitchen calendar. 'It's June the First today,' she told him. 'On the first day of the month you can make a wish. Go on.'

Matt closed his eyes and wished very hard. Up in his bedroom he'd just emptied his money-box pig and all he'd got out of it was seventy-five pence and three paper clips.

So he wished for a very small,
very cheap lion.

Mum went off to the sale very
early, to get her stall ready.

'I'm on the Coffee-and-Tea
stall,' she told him. 'People get
very thirsty at these sales. My
stall's right in the corner, by the
piano. Come and find me, when
you've had a look round.'

'When I've got my lion, you
mean,' Matt whispered and he
went off down the garden to
check that the shed was ready.
He'd bought a tin of Pretty Pussy
cat food for its first meal, just in
case it didn't like the half-
sausage, or the peanut butter
sandwich, and he'd only got fifty

pence left now. It would have to
be a real bargain lion, at this
rate.

At the bottom of the garden
there was a hole in the fence and
if he held his tummy in he could
just squeeze through. The hole
came out on the other side, near
the church hall dustbins. It was
Matt's secret passage.

When he'd stood up and
brushed the mud off his clothes he
went straight round to the front of
the church hall. The sale started
at two o'clock and he wanted to
be first in the queue, but there
were lots of people waiting
already.

He stared at them all in turn,
just to see if anybody looked like
the sort of person who might want
a lion. But it was all right. They
were mostly old women and old
men, clutching large plastic
carrier bags.

Matt felt happier. You couldn't
fit a lion into a carrier bag, not
even a small lion.

But why were all these people

coming to a jungle sale? Some of them looked as if they needed new trousers, new coats and new shoes. Not new pets. It was all a bit puzzling.

At two o'clock sharp, the church hall doors opened and the queue surged inside. Everyone seemed in a tremendous hurry and Matt was nearly knocked over as they all rushed about. The things for sale were set out on very high tables and he couldn't reach up.

All he saw were forests of trouser legs and knobbly pink knees.

'That's nice, Flo.'

Matt looked up. Mrs Biggs

from Number Nine was trying on
a huge purple hat with wavy
feathers.

'How much?'

'Ten pence to you, dear.'

'I'll take it.'

He began to feel quite hopeful.
Ten pence was cheap and purple
feathers meant purple birds.
There must be jungle things
around somewhere.

He gripped the edge of the
table and hauled himself up. 'Got
any lions?' he said.

'Sorry, dear, this is all hats. I've
a very nice Balaclava, it's hardly
been worn.'

'No thank you, I've already got
one of those. I'm really looking

for a lion,' and he moved on to the
next stall.

This one sold belts and shoes,
things made out of leather. Two
women were squabbling over a
great big handbag. 'I saw it first,'
one of them yelled. 'It's real
crocodile, this is.'

Matt looked down rather nervously. Crocodiles had very sharp teeth. But at least he'd not made a mistake. This was a jungle sale and if he couldn't buy a lion, perhaps he'd buy a tiny little crocodile instead. It could go in their garden pond, for a bit.

He pulled himself up again and rested his chin on the table. 'Have you got any lions?' he asked politely. 'Or a crocodile? Just a baby one?'

But the handbag lady glared at him. 'Go away,' she snapped. 'Go away with your silly questions. I'm extremely busy. Now then, Mr Blackett, yes, we do have some Wellingtons. What size?'

Matt slid to the floor again and wondered where to go next. He couldn't see Mum's Coffee-and-Tea stall and he couldn't see the jungle stalls either. All round him, people were pulling on jumpers and squeezing into skirts. One stall sold nothing but knickers and vests. An old lady got a whole bagful for twenty-five pence.

Things were certainly very cheap round here, but was it a jungle sale? He decided to find Mum and ask her where the animals were.

But as he was pushing his way through the crowds, towards her corner by the piano, he heard

something that stopped him in his tracks. 'White Elephant stall!' a lady was shouting, banging a tin lid to make everyone listen. 'This way to the White Elephant stall! Cheapest prices in town!'

Matt turned round and began to weave his way back through scratchy trousers and bony knees. An elephant stall would sell other jungle animals too. What a good job he'd heard in time.

Once more he stood on tiptoe so he could see the top of the table. But this time, before speaking to the stall lady, he had a very good look at everything first.

What a muddle!

The table was covered with

rubbish. Cups with no handles
and teapots with no spouts. A
blue toy rabbit with only one ear
and a red kettle with a great big
dent in it. All the things were
either broken completely or had
their most important bits missing.
As for 'white elephants'—there
just weren't any.

'Have you got any lions?' he whispered, though he knew the answer already. 'Have you got any animals at all?' Then he added rather fiercely, 'This is a white elephant stall, isn't it? You said so, when you banged the tin lid.'

The lady at the table peered down at him through her glasses. 'I'm very sorry,' she said kindly, 'but "white elephant" just means the things nobody really wants any more, the things that are no use to anyone. Of course, people do buy them sometimes, and glue them together. There's always a white elephant stall at a jumble sale. Now then, is there anything here you would like? It's all very cheap,' and she came round to the front of the stall to help him.

'Did you say JUMBLE sale?' Matt repeated in a very small voice. 'I thought it was going to be a JUNGLE sale. I'd come to buy a lion. I'd been saving up.' And he felt so disappointed that he collapsed on the floor in a heap, on a pile of old comics.

The white elephant lady bent down and helped him to his feet. 'We don't have any lions,' she explained, 'but we do have something else that might interest you. Come and see.'

Matt followed her round to the back of the stall.

'Look,' she said, opening a little wicker basket. 'I didn't put him out on the table, in case he got frightened.'

Matt looked. In the basket, curled up in a soft ginger ball, was a tiny kitten. It was snoring quietly.

'Nobody seems to want him,' said the stall lady sadly, 'and he's such a bargain. He's only fifty pence. It's a shame.'

Matt looked at the kitten for a very long time. 'I'll have him,' he said at last, digging down into his pocket. 'Cats are sort of lions, aren't they? And he's just the right colour.'

'He's called Scrap,' she told him, putting the five ten pences and the three paper clips into her money tin. 'I suppose it's because he's so little.'

Very quickly, before Mum spotted him, Matt picked up the wicker basket and carried it home through his secret hole in the

fence. Then he shut himself up in the garden shed, and let Scrap out.

Scrap loved the Pretty Pussy cat food, and the half-sausage, and the crisps and the peanut butter sandwich. In ten minutes flat he had gobbled up the whole lot. Then he lay on his back and waved his paws in the air while Matt tickled him. Then he chased his fat ginger tail round and round. Just watching him made you feel dizzy.

He didn't have to sleep in the garden shed after all. Mum liked him so much she let him curl up on the end of Matt's bed, to keep his toes warm. He was much

better than a hot water bottle
because he didn't go cold in the
middle of the night.

And they didn't call him Scrap because he was a very big eater. In fact, he grew up to be the biggest cat in the street. With his sharp claws and his sharp teeth and his great ginger face peering down at you out of a tree, he looked as good as a lion any day.

And that's what Matt called him, Lion. His secret wish had come true after all.